By Melissa Lagonegro
Illustrated by Niall Harding

First published by Parragon in 2012
Parragon
Queen Street House
4 Queen Street
Bath BA1 1HE, UK
www.parragon.com

ISBN 978-1-4454-4747-6

Printed in China

Ballerina Princess

A little story for little learners

PaRragon

Bath • New York • Singapore • Hong Kong • Cologne • Delhi
Melbourne • Amsterdam • Johannesburg • Auckland • Shenzhen

Snow White loves
to dream
about dancing.

6

She spins.

She twirls.

She moves
as if she is
floating on air.

Belle has sweet
dancing dreams.

Belle stands
on her toes.
She holds her
arms high.

She leaps
into the air.

Belle shines
like a star.
Her dress sparkles.

One leg is up.

One leg is down.

She holds her pose.

Aurora daydreams about her dancing costume.

Should she wear
a tutu or a gown?

Cinderella dances

at the royal ball

in her dreams.

She twirls and whirls
across the floor.

Prince Charming
watches Cinderella.

The Prince takes
her hand.
He asks her to dance.

They glide
across the room.
The guests
clap and cheer.

Ariel dreams
about dancing
with Prince Eric.
If only she had feet!

Spin and twirl
and jump!

Turn and leap
and prance!

A princess loves
to dance!